EEYORE FINDS
THE WOLERY

EEYORE FINDS
THE WOLERY

A. A. MILNE

illustrated by
ERNEST H. SHEPARD

TED SMART

EEYORE FINDS
THE WOLERY

Pooh had wandered into the Hundred Acre
Wood, and was standing in front of what had
once been Owl's House. It didn't look at all
like a house now; it looked like a tree
which had been blown down; and as soon as a
house looks like that, it is time you tried to
find another one. Pooh had had a Mysterious

Missage underneath his front door that morning,
saying, 'I AM SCERCHING FOR A NEW

HOUSE FOR OWL SO HAD YOU RABBIT,'
and while he was wondering what it meant
Rabbit had come in and read it for him.

'I'm leaving one for all the others,' said
Rabbit, 'and telling them what it means, and
they'll all search too. I'm in a hurry, good-bye.'
And he had run off.

Pooh followed slowly. He had something
better to do than to find a new house for Owl;
he had to make up a Pooh song about the old
one. Because he had promised Piglet days and
days ago that he would, and whenever he and
Piglet had met since, Piglet didn't actually say
anything, but you knew at once why he didn't;
and if anybody mentioned Hums or Trees or
String or Storms-in-the-Night, Piglet's nose
went all pink at the tip, and he talked about
something quite different in a hurried sort of
way.

'But it isn't Easy,' said Pooh to himself, as
he looked at what had once been Owl's House.
'Because Poetry and Hums aren't things which

you get, they're things which get *you*. And all you can do is to go where they can find you.'

He waited hopefully . . .

'Well,' said Pooh after a long wait, 'I shall begin "*Here lies a tree*" because it does, and then I'll see what happens.'

This is what happened:

Here lies a tree which Owl (a bird)
    Was fond of when it stood on end,
    And Owl was talking to a friend
Called Me (in case you hadn't heard)
When something Oo occurred.

For lo! the wind was blusterous
    And flattened out his favourite tree;
    And things looked bad for him and we—
Looked bad, I mean, for he and us—
I've never known them wuss.

Then Piglet (PIGLET) thought a thing:
    'Courage!' he said. 'There's always hope.
    I want a thinnish piece of rope.
Or, if there isn't any, bring
A thickish piece of string.'

So to the letter-box he rose,
    While Pooh and Owl said 'Oh!' and 'Hum!'
    And where the letters always come
(Called 'LETTERS ONLY') Piglet sqoze
His head and then his toes.

O gallant Piglet (PIGLET)! Ho!
    Did Piglet tremble? Did he blinch?
    No, no, he struggled inch by inch
Through LETTERS ONLY, as I know
Because I saw him go.

He ran and ran, and then he stood
    And shouted, 'Help for Owl, a bird,
    And Pooh, a bear!' until he heard
The others coming through the wood
As quickly as they could.

'Help-help and Rescue!' Piglet cried,
    And showed the others where to go.
    [Sing ho! for Piglet (PIGLET) ho!]
And soon the door was opened wide,
And we were both outside!

Sing ho! for Piglet, ho!
Ho!

'So there it is,' said Pooh, when he had sung this to himself three times. 'It's come different from what I thought it would, but it's come. Now I must go and sing it to Piglet.'

I AM SCERCHING FOR A NEW HOUSE FOR OWL SO HAD YOU RABBIT.

'What's all this?' said Eeyore.

Rabbit explained.

'What's the matter with his old house?'

Rabbit explained.

'Nobody tells me,' said Eeyore. 'Nobody keeps me informed. I make it seventeen days come Friday since anybody spoke to me.'

'It certainly isn't seventeen days—'

'Come Friday,' explained Eeyore.

'And to-day's Saturday,' said Rabbit. 'So that would make it eleven days. And I was here myself a week ago.'

'Not conversing,' said Eeyore. 'Not first one and then the other. You said "Hallo" and Flashed Past. I saw your tail a hundred yards up the hill as I was meditating my reply. I *had* thought of saying "What?" — but, of course, it was then too late.'

'Well, I was in a hurry.'

'No Give and Take,' Eeyore went on. 'No Exchange of Thought. "*Hallo—What*" — I mean, it gets you nowhere, particularly if the other person's tail is only just in sight for the second half of the conversation.'

'It's your fault, Eeyore. You've never been to see any of us. You just stay here in this one corner of the Forest waiting for the others to come to *you*. Why don't you go to *them* sometimes?'

Eeyore was silent for a little while, thinking.

'There may be something in what you say,
Rabbit,' he said at last. 'I have been
neglecting you. I must move about more.
I must come and go.'

'That's right, Eeyore. Drop in on any of
us at any time, when you feel like it.'

'Thank-you, Rabbit. And if anybody says in a Loud Voice "Bother, it's Eeyore" I can drop out again.'

Rabbit stood on one leg for a moment.

'Well,' he said, 'I must be going. I am rather busy this morning.'

'Good-bye,' said Eeyore.

'What? Oh, good-bye. And if you happen to come across a good house for Owl, you must let us know.'

'I will give my mind to it,' said Eeyore.

Rabbit went.

Pooh had found Piglet, and they were walking back to the Hundred Acre Wood together.

'Piglet,' said Pooh a little shyly, after they had walked for some time without saying anything.

'Yes, Pooh?'

'Do you remember when I said that a Respectful Pooh Song might be written about You Know What?'

'Did you, Pooh?' said Piglet, getting
a little pink round the nose. 'Oh, yes, I
believe you did.'

'It's been written, Piglet.'

The pink went slowly up Piglet's nose to
his ears, and settled there.

'Has it, Pooh?' he asked huskily. 'About—
about—That Time When?—Do you mean
really written?'

'Yes, Piglet.'

The tips of Piglet's ears glowed suddenly,
and he tried to say something; but even after
he had husked once or twice, nothing came
out. So Pooh went on:

'There are seven verses in it.'

'Seven?' said Piglet as carelessly as he
could. 'You don't often get *seven* verses in
a Hum, do you, Pooh?'

'Never,' said Pooh. 'I don't suppose it's
ever been heard of before.'

'Do the Others know yet?' asked Piglet,
stopping for a moment to pick up a stick and

throw it away.

'No,' said Pooh. 'And I wondered which you would like best: for me to hum it now, or to wait till we find the others, and then hum it to all of you?'

Piglet thought for a little.

'I think what I'd like best, Pooh, is I'd like you to hum it to me *now*—and—and *then* to hum it to all of us. Because then Everybody would hear it, but I could say "Oh, yes, Pooh's told me" and pretend not to be listening.'

So Pooh hummed it to him, all the seven verses, and Piglet said nothing, but just stood and glowed. For never before had anyone sung ho for Piglet (PIGLET) ho all by himself. When it was over, he wanted to ask for one of the verses over again, but didn't quite like to. It was the verse beginning 'O gallant Piglet,' and it seemed to him a very thoughtful way of beginning a piece of poetry.

'Did I really do all that?' he said at last.

'Well,' said Pooh, 'in poetry—in a piece of poetry—well, you *did* it, Piglet, because the poetry says you did. And that's how people know.'

'Oh!' said Piglet. 'Because I—I thought I did blinch a little. Just at first. And it says, "Did he blinch no no." That's why.'

'You only blinched inside,' said Pooh, 'and that's the bravest way for a Very Small Animal not to blinch that there is.'

Piglet sighed with happiness, and began to think about himself. He was BRAVE. . . .

When they got to Owl's old house, they found everybody else there except Eeyore.

Christopher Robin was telling them what to do, and Rabbit was telling them again directly afterwards, in case they hadn't heard, and then they were all doing it. They had got a rope and were pulling Owl's chairs and pictures and things out of his old house so as to be ready to put them into his new one. Kanga was down below tying the things on, and calling out to Owl, 'You won't want this dirty old dish-cloth any more, will you, and what

about this carpet, it's all in holes,' and Owl
was calling back indignantly, 'Of course I
do! It's just a question of arranging the
furniture properly, and it isn't a dish-cloth,
it's my shawl.' Every now and then Roo fell in
and came back on the rope with the next article,
which flustered Kanga a little because she never
knew where to look for him. So she got cross
with Owl and said that his house was a Disgrace,
all damp and dirty, and it was quite time it

did tumble down. Look at that horrid bunch
of toadstools growing out of the corner there?
So Owl looked down, a little surprised because he
didn't know about this, and then gave a short
sarcastic laugh, and explained that this was his
sponge, and that if people didn't know a perfectly
ordinary bath-sponge when they saw it,
things were coming to a pretty pass.
'*Well*!' said Kanga, and Roo fell in quickly,
crying 'I *must* see Owl's sponge!
Oh, there it is! Oh, Owl! Owl,
it isn't a sponge, it's a spudge!
Do you know what a spudge is, Owl?
It's when your sponge gets all —'
and Kanga **said**, 'Roo, dear!' very quickly,
because that's *not* the way to talk to anybody
who can spell TUESDAY.

But they were all quite happy when Pooh and
Piglet came along, and they stopped working in
order to have a little rest and listen to

Pooh's new song. So then they all told Pooh
how good it was, and Piglet said carelessly,
'It *is* good, isn't it? I mean as a song.'

'And what about the new house?' asked
Pooh. 'Have you found it, Owl?'

'He's found a name for it,' said Christopher
Robin, lazily nibbling at a piece of grass,
'so now all he wants is the house.'

'I am calling it this,' said Owl importantly, and he showed them what he had been making. It was a square piece of board with the name of the house painted on it:

THE WOLERY

It was at this exciting moment that something came through the trees, and bumped into Owl. The board fell to the ground, and Piglet and Roo bent over it eagerly.

'Oh, it's you,' said Owl crossly.

'Hallo, Eeyore!' said Rabbit. '*There* you are!
Where have *you* been?'

Eeyore took no notice of them.

'Good morning, Christopher Robin,' he said,
brushing away Roo and Piglet, and sitting down
on THE WOLERY. 'Are we alone?'

'Yes,' said Christopher Robin, smiling
to himself.

'I have been told—the news has worked through to my corner of the Forest—the damp bit down on the right which nobody wants—that a certain Person is looking for a house. I have found one for him.'

'Ah, well done,' said Rabbit kindly.

Eeyore looked round slowly at him, and then turned back to Christopher Robin.

'We have been joined by something,' he said, in a loud whisper. 'But no matter. We can leave it behind. If you will come with me, Christopher Robin, I will show you the house.'

Christopher Robin jumped up.

'Come on, Pooh,' he said.

'Come on, Tigger!' cried Roo.

'Shall we go, Owl?' said Rabbit.

'Wait a moment,' said Owl, picking up his notice-board, which had just come into sight again.

Eeyore waved them back.

'Christopher Robin and I are going for

a Short Walk,' he said, 'not a Jostle. If he
likes to bring Pooh and Piglet with him, I shall
be glad of their company, but one must
be able to Breathe.'

'That's all right,' said Rabbit, rather glad
to be left in charge of something.
'We'll go on getting the things out.

Now then, Tigger, where's that rope? What's the matter, Owl?'

Owl, who had just discovered that his new address was THE SMEAR, coughed at Eeyore sternly, but said nothing, and Eeyore, with most of THE WOLERY behind him, marched off with his friends.

So, in a little while, they came to the house which Eeyore had found, and just before they came to it, Piglet was nudging Pooh, and Pooh was nudging Piglet, and they were saying, 'It is!' and 'It can't be!' and 'It is, *really!*' to each other.

And when they got there, it really was.

'There!' said Eeyore proudly, stopping them outside Piglet's house. 'And the name on it, and everything!'

'Oh!' cried Christopher Robin, wondering whether to laugh or what.

'Just the house for Owl. Don't you think so, little Piglet?'

And then Piglet did a Noble Thing, and he did it in a sort of dream, while he was thinking of all the wonderful words Pooh had hummed about him.

'Yes, it's just the house for Owl,' he said grandly. 'And I hope he'll be very happy in it.' And then he gulped twice, because he had been very happy in it himself.

'What do *you* think, Christopher Robin?' asked Eeyore a little anxiously, feeling that something wasn't quite right.

Christopher Robin had a question to ask first, and he was wondering how to ask it.

'Well,' he said at last, 'it's a very nice house, and if your own house is blown down, you *must* go somewhere else, mustn't you, Piglet? What would *you* do, if *your* house was blown down?'

Before Piglet could think, Pooh answered for him.

'He'd come and live with me,' said Pooh, 'wouldn't you, Piglet?'

Piglet squeezed his paw.

'Thank you, Pooh,' he said, 'I should love to.'

Eeyore finds the Wolery
is taken from *The House at Pooh Corner*
originally published in Great Britain 11th October 1928
by Methuen & Co. Ltd.
Text by A.A.Milne and line drawings by Ernest H.Shepard
copyright under the Berne Convention

First published 1991 by Methuen Children's Books
an imprint of Egmont Children's Books Limited
239 Kensington High Street, London W8 6SA

This edition first produced in 1998 for The Book People
Hall Wood Avenue, Haydock, St Helens WA11 9UL

ISBN 1 85613 449 0

3 5 7 9 10 8 6 4

Printed in Hong Kong